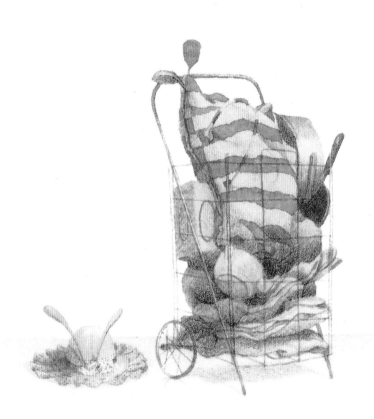

MR. KNEEBON

To Mary Lou, with affection
To Jessie (Yum. Yum.)

Canadian Cataloguing in Publication Data

Wallace, Ian, 1950–
Mr. Kneebone's new digs

ISBN 0-88899-143-6

I. Title.

PS8595.A5857M7 1991   jC813'.54   C91-093792-3
PZ7.W34Mr 1991

A Groundwood Book
Douglas & McIntyre Ltd.
585 Bloor Street West
Toronto, Ontario M6G 1K5

Design by Michael Solomon
Printed and bound in Hong Kong
by Everbest Printing Co. Ltd.

E'S NEW DIGS

WRITTEN AND ILLUSTRATED BY

IAN WALLACE

A
GROUNDWOOD
BOOK ℅ 1991

Douglas & McIntyre
TORONTO/VANCOUVER

Mr. Kneebone sat in the window of the room he shared with April Moth. He was hoping for a breeze from the alley. But nothing stirred that steamy summer morning except April Moth, who was darting about the room killing flies.

Thwack. Thwack. Thwack. One by one they tumbled to the floor.

With a loud *haaarrruuummmppphhh*, April Moth plunked herself down in a chair and dropped one fly after another into her best friend's mouth.

"Good ol' boy," she said and scratched his ears.

Crunch. Crunch. Crunch. A sound crackled through the room.

Mr. Kneebone and April Moth looked toward the curtained cupboard beneath the sink.

Crunch. Crunch. Crunch.

April Moth flung back the curtain. A rat stared out, its mouth full of macaroni.

Thwack. April Moth's fly swatter came down across its nose.

The rat leaped onto the floor. Quick as a wink, Mr. Kneebone snatched it up by its tail.

April Moth cried out, "Sixty rats in six nights! We can endure ninety-five pesky flies a day, but we'll not suffer rats another night."

She pulled their bundle buggy from a dingy closet and packed it with everything they owned. Sink cupboards and drawers were emptied of odds and ends, blankets, a tea pot and frying pan.

Then, donning her cheeriest hat, April Moth ushered Mr. Kneebone out the door and slammed it behind her.

Kerplunk. Kerplunk. Kerplunk. Their bundle buggy went down five flights of stairs to the landlady's door. Mr. Kneebone carried the rat in his teeth.

"Are you there, Mrs. Bataloon?"

"Whaddayawan'?" boomed a dark voice.

"Just a moment of your time. It's April Moth and Mr. Kneebone."

The door banged open and an enormous woman appeared. She held a fork in one hand while balancing a plate piled high with spaghetti and meatballs in the other.

"Whaddayawan'fromme, Aprilmoff?" screeched Mrs. Bataloon.

"Over the past few months winter chills have whistled through our broken windows. Spring rains dripping from the ceiling have made puddles in my shoes and on Mr. Kneebone while he slept. There have been frozen pipes, no heat and soaring heat, flies flying through holes in our screens large enough for an airplane. But this is the last straw!" April Moth bent down and took the rat from Mr. Kneebone. She smacked it dead centre in the spaghetti.

The plate smashed onto the floor. Meatballs rolled as the frightened rat scurried off, *skitteree, skitteree, skitteree.*

April Moth hung the room key on the tines of Mrs. Bataloon's fork and strode out the front door with Mr. Kneebone at her heels.

"Now," she assured him, "we'll find new digs that are truly fine."

Kerplunk. Kerplunk. Kerplunk.

Down the stone steps they went and into the bustling street. The buggy's wheels clattered higglety-pigglety on the sidewalk. Four blocks east and three blocks south stood a ten-storey building. A sign posted in the window read:

ROOM FOR RENT

$5 A NIGHT

APPLY AT YOUR OWN RISK

The flowers had been bitten off a plant that sat on the window ledge.

''All the screens are torn,'' said April Moth.

'E'gads,' worried Mr. Kneebone.

Kerplunk. Kerplunk. Kerplunk. They marched up the stone steps and through the front door. A foul odour caught them by surprise.

'CATS!' barked Mr. Kneebone. A moment later he spotted their eyes—ever so faint at first, then sparkling brighter.

''Multi-coloured eyes,'' whispered April Moth. ''Too many to count.''

'Of CATS. Ge-zillions of CATS!' barked Mr. Kneebone. So many pointy teeth. So many fierce claws.

He hugged April Moth's side as cats showered down on them, big ones that weighed twenty pounds or more, long-boned mean ones, grey dappled, calico, marbled, and white-booted ones. Cats seeped out of every doorway. They prowled down the staircase from the floors above.

'Meeeee-e-e-e-eo-o-o-o-w,' they yowled in unison.

'Meeeee-e-e-e-eo-o-o-o-w,' they whined.

''Be gone,'' cried April Moth.

The cats just slunk past Mr. Kneebone, biding their time; so close that their fur brushed his face, his back, his legs. He growled and snapped at any cat who dared come too near.

With a quick turn of the bundle buggy, April Moth headed for the front door. Mr. Kneebone bolted to safety and the street once again.

April Moth scratched his ears. ''We could never live in digs like that, ol' boy. Why, did you get a whiff of the sickly cat stew? Peew!''

Kerplunk. Kerplunk. Kerplunk.

On they trudged. There were no rooms that they could afford. April Moth grew weary beneath the sun that baked her back. Mr. Kneebone's tongue felt parched and dry.

They stopped by a grocer's stand. There were so many delicious things to eat: oranges, apples, pears and plums.

'Lunch,' barked Mr. Kneebone.

''Oranges,'' said April Moth. ''Your favourite, so rare and tasty and good.'' She peeled one and packed the other in her buggy.

Across the street a guitarist played while they ate.

''Come along, look up, be happy . . .'' he sang. ''Look to where the grass grows green.''

April Moth could not resist the musician's call. She kicked up her heels and clapped her hands to the rhythmic beat. Then she jigged across the busy road. Mr. Kneebone jigged after her. When she reached the young man's side, she dropped an orange section into the hat at his feet.

He thanked her with a nod of his head.

''Come along, look up, be happy. Look to where the sun does shine.''

April Moth looked up. There before her eyes hung a weathered sign. It read: OL RIVER OTEL. And underneath, QUIET(?) ROO TO LET. $3 ER DAY.

Kerplunk. Kerplunk. Kerplunk.

"We'd like to see a room," announced April Moth to a man they met just inside the lobby door.

"O fer sure. O fer sure. O fer sure. Sweet Daddy Three Times is the name," he said, and pointed to Mr. Kneebone. "Cool cat, cool cat, cool cat."

"Cool *dog*. Cool *dog*. Cool *dog*," replied April Moth.

Sweet Daddy laughed and shook his head. April Moth and Mr. Kneebone followed him down the hall.

"Here we are. Here we are. Here we are," he chimed.

The room was as ragged as a scarecrow's hat and seemed to sag as they entered. They checked under the lumpy bed and inside the closet for rat holes.

"Only two."

April Moth opened the bureau drawer and ran her finger inside. "Fil-thee."

She turned on the sink faucets to let the water run; first hot, drip, drip, then cold, drip, drip, then both together, *sputter, sputter, sputter-r-rspree-e-e.*

Just then they heard a few sharp plinks, then several neat glinks, followed by a long mournful wail. A quarter note brought a wall of sound, loud and red and hot as salsa sauce. The noise tingled down the bed springs . . . *pe-toom, pe-toom, pe-toom* . . . and jingled on the door- knobs . . . *chittle-e-e-e, chittle-e-e-e, chittle-e-e-e* . . . and bounced off the windows, *good little baby, good little me.*

Sweet Daddy shrugged his shoulders. "Can you dig it all day? Can you dig it all night? Can you dig it, April Moth?"

With her fingers in her ears, April Moth looked down at Mr. Kneebone. Regretfully they shook their heads three times.

"Too bad, sweet sister. Too bad, good brother. But if it gets cold outside, come back, come back, come back."

Kerplunk. Kerplunk. Kerplunk.

Outside again they headed farther east.

"We're certain to find new digs by nightfall," April Moth assured Mr. Kneebone with a warm pat on his back. But as they walked, the buildings around them grew taller—banks, offices and stores, but nowhere to live.

After an hour April Moth plunked herself down on a cement bench and took off her hat. Mr. Kneebone ran up beside her.

"Good ol' boy," she said and scratched his ears. "What can we do?" People, alone and in couples, rushed past heading for home. Cars whizzed by and the pavement grew hotter. Mr. Kneebone nuzzled April Moth's arm. He had a stick in his mouth.

'Toss. Toss. Toss,' he barked.

April Moth thought she was going to cry, but she tossed the stick instead, watching it arc through the air and listening to Mr. Kneebone's claws click after it.

"We need grass!" she cried out. "Where a dog can fetch and run." She tossed the stick again, *click, click, click,* and suddenly the answer came to her.

She gathered up her hat, the buggy and Mr. Kneebone in such a hurry that she was halfway down the block before she realized she was singing to herself.

"Come along, look up, be happy. Look to where the grass grows green."

She ran, dragging the cart behind her, to a gate she remembered from long ago. Turning their backs on the city, she and Mr. Kneebone headed down a trail that led gently into a park. The air was cooler under the trees.

When they reached a broad meadow at the bottom of the valley, April Moth kicked off her shoes and socks and ran barefoot beside Mr. Kneebone.

"We won't find any rats here!" sang April Moth. "Why, just breathe that fresh night air."

She wheeled their bundle buggy through the sea of grass, *sha-a-loon, sha-a-loon, sha-a-loon*. And there as if it had been waiting for them was a small cave with walls one-storey high. A space just large enough for a Moth and her dog.

"We've found our new digs," they cheered.

April Moth tossed her hat in the air. While Mr. Kneebone raced to bring it back, she sat on the ground. It felt cool beneath her tired legs. She pulled the second orange out of her bundle buggy and peeled it.

As they ate, the evening air exploded with fireflies.

'Yum. Yum. Yum,' barked Mr. Kneebone. 'Hot flies.'